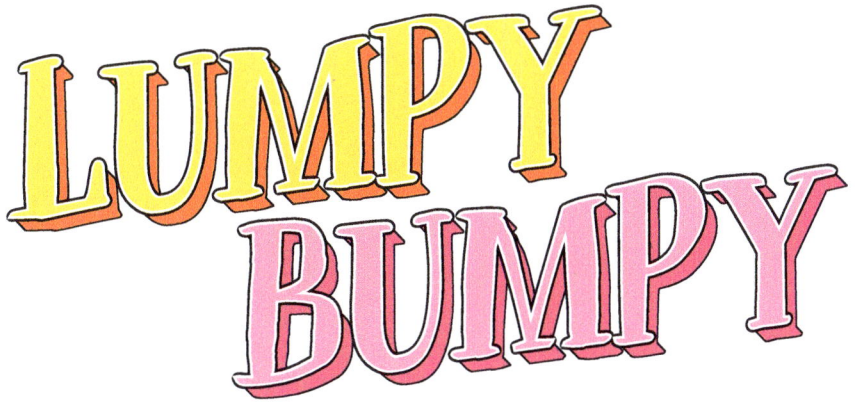

Arline M. Taborek

Lumpy Bumpy
Copyright © 2016 by Arline M. Taborek. All rights reserved.

This title is also available as a Tate Out Loud product. Visit www.tatepublishing.com for more information.

No part of this publication may be reproduced, stored in a retrieval system or transmitted in any way by any means, electronic, mechanical, photocopy, recording or otherwise without the prior permission of the author except as provided by USA copyright law.

The opinions expressed by the author are not necessarily those of Tate Publishing, LLC.

This novel is a work of fiction. Names, descriptions, entities, and incidents included in the story are products of the author's imagination. Any resemblance to actual persons, events, and entities is entirely coincidental.

Published by Tate Publishing & Enterprises, LLC
127 E. Trade Center Terrace | Mustang, Oklahoma 73064 USA
1.888.361.9473 | www.tatepublishing.com

Tate Publishing is committed to excellence in the publishing industry. The company reflects the philosophy established by the founders, based on Psalm 68:11,
"The Lord gave the word and great was the company of those who published it."

Book design copyright © 2016 by Tate Publishing, LLC. All rights reserved.
Cover and interior design by Ralph Lim
Illustrations by Bea may Ybanez

Published in the United States of America

ISBN: 978-1-68270-669-5
1. Juvenile Fiction / Family / Multigenerational
2. Juvenile Fiction / Imagination & Play
16.08.01

My sweet granddaughter Shaylee's endearing antics inspired me to write this story about a special moment in both our lives.

All my love to you, Shaylee,

Nana

There is a Lumpy Bumpy on the floor.

It's right outside my bedroom door.

The Lumpy Bumpy is covered in a fluffy blanket, I see.

I wonder who this Lumpy Bumpy could be.

I don't know from where this Lumpy Bumpy came.

Is it a girl? Is it a boy? Does this Lumpy Bumpy have a name?

Oh, wait, I just heard a sound!

It's coming from the Lumpy Bumpy on the ground.

As I'm watching, the blanket starts to move slowly like a worm.

All of a sudden this Lumpy Bumpy starts to squirm.

I walk around this Lumpy Bumpy, poking it lightly with my foot.

Looking for a way to peek inside and somehow get a look.

I lift a corner of the blanket to look underneath, but all I *see* is black.

Then that Lumpy Bumpy rolls away and grabs the blanket back!

All of a sudden, out pops a foot that stretches into the air.

A moment later, a second foot sticks out and now there is a pair.

The blanket rises in a whoosh as the Lumpy Bumpy thrashes about.

It seems like that Lumpy Bumpy is trying to get out.

In a cautious voice, I say, "Come out so we can play."

But the Lumpy Bumpy does not listen and slowly crawls away.

I follow the Lumpy Bumpy and try to give the blanket a tug.

Then that Lumpy Bumpy jumps up with the blanket on its head and runs across the rug.

So I chase the Lumpy Bumpy down the hall and through a door.

I finally catch that Lumpy Bumpy, and I tackle it to the floor.

Hearing giggles, I pull off the fluffy blanket and laugh because then I knew.

That the squirmy Lumpy Bumpy is really only you!

The End

listen|imagine|view|experience

AUDIO BOOK DOWNLOAD INCLUDED WITH THIS BOOK!

In your hands you hold a complete digital entertainment package. In addition to the paper version, you receive a free download of the audio version of this book. Simply use the code listed below when visiting our website. Once downloaded to your computer, you can listen to the book through your computer's speakers, burn it to an audio CD or save the file to your portable music device (such as Apple's popular iPod) and listen on the go!

How to get your free audio book digital download:

1. Visit www.tatepublishing.com and click on the e|LIVE logo on the home page.
2. Enter the following coupon code:
   10fa-9723-3fb6-4af4-b6ce-8316-d0bc-2eca
3. Download the audio book from your e|LIVE digital locker and begin enjoying your new digital entertainment package today!

CPSIA information can be obtained
at www.ICGtesting.com
Printed in the USA
LVOW05s1041121116
512353LV00016B/87/P